DRAGON REALM

••••••••••••••••••••••••••••••••

celebrated

World Book Day 2023
with this gift from
my local bookseller and
Simon & Schuster Children's Books.

A DRAGON REALM

ADVENTURE

SIMON & SCHUSTER

For Rachel and Amina,
who always make sure our dragons soar

First published in Great Britain in 2023 by Simon & Schuster UK Ltd

Copyright © 2023 Katherine Webber Tsang and Kevin Tsang

1 3 5 7 9 10 8 6 4 2

Simon & Schuster UK Ltd
1st Floor, 222 Gray's Inn Road
London WC1X 8HB

www.simonandschuster.co.uk
www.simonandschuster.com.au
www.simonandschuster.co.in

Simon & Schuster Australia, Sydney
Simon & Schuster India, New Delhi

A CIP catalogue record for this book is available from the British Library.

PB ISBN 978-1-3985-2309-8
eBook ISBN 978-1-3985-2310-4
eAudio ISBN 978-1-3985-2325-8

Typeset in Garamond by M Rules
Printed and bound using 100% Renewable
Electricity at CPI Group (UK) Ltd

WORLD BOOK DAY®

World Book Day's mission is to offer every
child and young person the opportunity to
read and love books by giving you the chance
to have a book of your own.

To find out more, and for fun activities including
the monthly World Book Day Book Club, video
stories and book recommendations, visit
worldbookday.com

World Book Day is a charity sponsored by
National Book Tokens.

Soaring

Billy Chan soared through the sky on the back of his dragon.

Riding Spark, his heart-bonded dragon, was endlessly thrilling. He'd never forget the first time they'd flown together, and he'd never take for granted how effortless it was now.

Once upon a time, dragons had just been a fantasy to him. And even after he'd discovered Dragon Mountain and met Spark, he'd never imagined flying in broad daylight in the Human Realm. Until very recently, few people had known that dragons even existed, let alone that they had their own separate realm. But now they were here, in the same world as humans.

Billy had seen a lot of dragons, but he was certain Spark was the most majestic of them all. She had shimmery blue scales flecked with gold and sharp gold antlers that twisted back from her diamond-shaped head. She had a long neck, almost like a swan, that curved into her powerful seahorse-like body. An electric blue mane ran from her head all along her spine to the end of her tail. And she had huge, almost translucent wings to keep her airborne. Spark was a seer dragon, meaning she sometimes saw visions of the future, but she also had the power of electricity and ice. Because of this, she seemed to emit her own light, and the air around her crackled with power.

When twelve-year-old Billy had first seen Spark, deep in Dragon Mountain, he'd felt immediately drawn towards her, although he hadn't known they were destined to be heart-bonded. A heart bond only happened if a dragon found a human who had a heart that matched their own. Both the human and the dragon gained power through their bond, and they would be forever linked, as Billy and Spark were. A heart bond was the strongest way for a dragon to gain power.

Billy, a Chinese-American surfer from San Francisco, California, used to think the most exciting thing that would ever happen to him was winning the local surfing championships. But he'd never forgotten the bedtime stories his dad, who was from Hong Kong, told him and his brother about these mythical creatures, and when Billy had been sent to summer camp in China to study language and culture, something extraordinary had happened.

Together with his new friends Ling-Fei, Charlotte and Dylan, they had opened Dragon Mountain that loomed behind the camp. Inside, Spark and three other magical warrior dragons were trapped. Each of them had a different strength and skill, and each of them had heart-bonded with one of the children. The enormous red warrior dragon,

Tank, had connected with Charlotte from Atlanta. Curious, kind and green-hued Buttons, a healer dragon, had found a heart bond with Irish Dylan. And the sassy and sarcastic Xing, a speedy silver seeker dragon, had bonded with Ling-Fei, who was from a small village in China.

Billy and his friends had freed the dragons and followed them into their realm. Using their newfound powers, they defeated the fearsome Dragon of Death who wanted to rule both humans and dragons. After that, Billy and his friends returned to their home, and the dragons to theirs.

But then dragons and other creatures began to appear in the Human Realm, bringing new dangers and new enemies. Billy and his friends banded together again to protect both realms. Along the way, they made new friends, including Jordan Edwards, a Black British boy who had accidentally stumbled into the Dragon Realm, and Lola Lam, a Chinese-Hawaiian girl who had been one of the first to see a dragon appear in the Human Realm.

So Billy and Spark had been through a lot together before they found themselves soaring over London. They were on a new mission, and Billy felt the thrill of it thrumming in his blood. Whenever he was with Spark and his fellow dragon-riders, he felt invincible, which was a good thing, given what they were up against.

Because the Dragon Realm, and all the mythical beasts that lived there, was crashing into the Human Realm. Every day something new burst through, falling from the sky, popping up from underground or emerging from the sea.

And it wasn't just dragons. Dragons had a tentative peace with humans, and even the new arrivals honoured it. The legendary Glorious Old, the only dragon who had the power to communicate with every one of her kind, had brokered that peace. But even she couldn't control the other creatures from the wilds of Dragon Realm which now found themselves in the human world.

And some of those creatures were extremely

unhappy to be there. Like the giant glowing scorpion with two stingers that had landed in the middle of Trafalgar Square.

Billy and Spark, along with Jordan on his dragon Midnight and Ling-Fei on her dragon Xing, raced towards the chaos. As the scorpion came into view, Billy groaned. He had been hoping it would be an easy job battling the scorpion, but as soon as he saw it, he knew the creature wasn't going anywhere without a fight.

It was massive, its body the size of a double-decker bus. It waved its two stingers, knocking into nearby buildings.

And it was angry.

Very angry.

Supercharged

Hope you're ready, Billy thought down his dragon bond to Spark. *That thing looks lethal.*

Billy loved a lot of things about having a heart bond with a dragon, but something he always found extra special was that he and Spark could speak directly into each other's minds through their bond.

It is, Spark thought back, and in his mind, Billy heard dry amusement mixed with genuine wariness in her tone. *I avoided these creatures in the Dragon Realm, and with good reason. This is no ordinary scorpion.*

I can see that, Billy thought back. *It's as big as a bus! And it has TWO stingers!*

Not only that. It can shoot venom from both its tails, and it has regenerative powers, Spark replied down the bond.

Meaning . . . ? Billy asked.

Meaning it will be very difficult to get close to it, and even harder to subdue it.

Billy gulped. If Spark, the bravest and most powerful dragon he knew, was nervous, this really was going to be a challenge!

Billy looked over his shoulder to make sure Jordan and Ling-Fei were close behind. He knew he couldn't take on this scorpion without them. It felt a little strange to see their group down to three when they had so recently been six. But the friends were needed all over the world, so they'd decided that Billy, Jordan and Ling-Fei would stay in London, where the rip between realms was causing the most activity. Charlotte, Dylan and Lola would travel to other locations where creatures were coming through.

As Dylan had said, 'Even one dragon was an abnormal number', but for some mysterious reason, certain places seemed to be hotspots for unwanted arrivals from the Dragon Realm.

Billy smiled at Jordan, who waved at him from his own dragon, Midnight. Billy and Jordan had met not long ago when Jordan followed his scientist mother into the Dragon Realm. Professor Edwards had been working for a top-secret organization called TURBO, and when she'd found out that her unscrupulous boss, Frank Albert, had entered the Dragon Realm and was using magical properties found in it for evil, she went to stop him. But by the time they'd located him, Frank had already acquired the *sanguinem gladio*, the legendary Blood Sword that could cut through anything, including between realms.

In his greed to seek out the powerful golden elixir that gave power to people and objects, Frank Albert carelessly sliced through the realms, weakening the boundary between them. The result was that the Dragon Realm started to fall into the Human Realm, and now there was no turning back. There would soon only be one realm – a realm where humans and dragons were going to have to live together peacefully in the modern world.

So Billy and his friends were currently acting as 'supercharged pest control' to subdue the confused creatures that were appearing in the Human Realm. Sometimes a dragon without a human heart bond would help, but despite Glorious Old's call for peace, few of them had much interest. Spark believed that dragons would start caring more when they found their own human heart bonds, but until then it was up to Billy and the group.

Luckily, this wasn't their first time battling a supercharged pest. If anything, Jordan and Midnight looked eager to take on the scorpion. Jordan was leaning forward, urging his dragon on even faster, and Midnight's horns were already glowing a molten orange, a sure sign she was ready for battle. She was a young dragon with shining midnight blue scales and enormous twisting horns that glowed bright orange when she lost her temper or got fired up. Because Midnight was a fledgling, she was still discovering all her strengths, but so far, they knew she could zap things with her horns, send out huge blasts of power and create protective invisibility shields.

Just ahead of Jordan and Midnight were Ling-Fei and Xing. Xing was slicing through the sky so fast she was a silver blur, her long slender serpent-like body glinting in the sunlight. Xing was the fastest dragon Billy had ever seen. Her speed and her sparkling silver scales had inspired her name, which meant 'star' in Mandarin. In addition to her speed, she had power over water and could use her magic to do all kinds of enchantments. Billy was glad to have her on his side.

And the dragons weren't the only ones with powers. When the children had formed their heart bonds, they had gained superpowers of their own. Billy had super speed and super agility, which meant he could climb walls and sense movement.

Best of all, he could channel power from Spark, giving him the ability to create electric shields and even travel through electric currents.

Ling-Fei was connected to nature. She could communicate with the earth itself, and sense life and magic. Billy had seen her pull off truly incredible feats, such as when she'd opened the earth by sheer force of will. She could also sense the emotions of living creatures and even find the spirits sleeping inside rivers and mountains.

And Jordan ... Well, if Billy was honest with himself, he was a little envious of his ability. Jordan could *teleport*. And not just himself: he could teleport anyone who he was touching. He'd only done it a few times, and only for short distances, but it was extremely useful and super cool.

Billy also found himself wishing that they had Charlotte's super strength, Dylan's charm, or Lola's ability to slow down time to take on the scorpion. Because it had sensed them, and with a terrifying screech, it attacked.

Billy had battled a scorpion before, in the Frozen Wasteland of the Dragon Realm, though that one had been merely man-sized, not bus-sized. Ling-Fei must have remembered, because as Xing flew close to Spark, she called out. 'This should be easy, Billy! You've done it before!' She gave him an encouraging grin.

'Not like this,' Billy yelled back as the huge scorpion raised both its stingers and shot out streams of venom. The dragons dodged, but Billy winced as the venom hit the pavement and burned holes in it. Sizzling steam rose up making Billy's eyes water even at a distance.

'I do *not* like this scorpion!' Midnight declared, dancing anxiously in the air. 'Maybe we can find someone else to battle it?'

Jordan reached out and stroked Midnight soothingly on the head. 'We can do this, Midnight. We'll be okay!' Then he looked up at Billy and Ling-Fei. 'Right?'

'I hope so,' Billy called over, scanning the ground to make sure there weren't any bystanders.

Luckily it seemed everyone had very sensibly cleared out. 'We have to make sure we contain the scorpion in the square!'

The scorpion screeched again and squirted out more venom, this time directly at Midnight and Jordan.

'Why is it so angry?' Jordan shouted as Midnight dodged the spray.

'I'm trying to calm it!' Ling-Fei cried back. 'But it doesn't have thoughts, just anger and fear ... and something that feels like hunger?'

'Oh, great,' said Billy sarcastically, cringing as the scorpion thwacked its tail so hard on the ground that the entire street cracked. 'So after it knocks us out of the sky, it might eat us for dinner.'

'Not today, mate!' said Jordan, just as the scorpion reared up on its back legs and lunged at Midnight with one of its front pincers. It was so big it could crush the dragon easily, and for one sickening moment, Billy thought that Jordan and Midnight were done for. But then, in a flash of light, they appeared directly below Billy and Spark.

Jordan's eyes were wide. 'Whew! I'm still getting used to teleporting! That was close!'

'Too close,' agreed Midnight.

'We can evade the scorpion all day, but we have to defeat it,' said Billy. 'Spark! Send out an electric blast.'

Spark fired electricity at the huge scorpion, and, for a moment it went still, clearly stunned. But a second later, it screeched even louder and shot a stream of venom that narrowly missed the group.

'Odious creature,' muttered Xing. 'Let me show it how to behave! Ling-Fei, hold on!' With a whoosh, Xing flew directly towards the scorpion's head. Ling-Fei's long black braids whipped out behind her, and her usual smile was replaced by a look of tense concentration.

The scorpion, still slightly dazed by Spark's lightning attack, tried to knock Xing and Ling-Fei out of the air with its pincers, but Xing was too fast. She flew even closer until she was directly between its two front-facing eyes. Then, to Billy's horror and amazement, Ling-Fei stood up on Xing's back, reached out and put her hand on the scorpion's forehead.

For a moment it seemed that Ling-Fei and Xing had put the scorpion in a trance. It began to sway like it might topple over, but then it recovered and let out an ear-splitting hiss before aiming both stingers directly at Ling-Fei and Xing.

'NO!' Billy cried. 'Spark, quick! SUPERCHARGE ME!' A jolt of energy shot through him right before he leaped off Spark, directly towards the back of the scorpion.

Falling Fireballs

Billy landed in a crouch on the scorpion's armoured back. His whole body was thrumming with electricity, so much so that it looked like he was wearing a sparking, crackling suit made of lightning.

Right as he landed, Xing zigzagged, narrowly avoiding the scorpion's deadly sharp stinger, still glistening with venom. But the scorpion wasn't interested in the dragon now. Billy sent pulse after pulse of electric current from his hands into the creature's back. It screeched and tried to use its stinger to knock Billy off, and when that didn't work, it began to buck like a bronco.

Billy held on, his hands buzzing with jolts as he gripped the grooves in the monstrous scorpion's back. He and his friends were going to win, whatever it took.

Spark! Can you help me out? Billy thought as he flipped right onto the scorpion's head. The last time he'd battled a scorpion, he'd tricked it into impaling itself with its own stinger, but he didn't think that would work with this one.

Of course, Spark thought back. *I'll attack.*

A moment later, the scorpion levitated with the power of Spark's blast. Billy felt the waves of electricity ricochet through its body.

I do not want to kill it, Spark thought. *Only weaken and subdue it. Then we can move it elsewhere. We cannot blame it for being angry and afraid. It does not want to be here.*

Where will we move it? Billy thought back. *It isn't exactly small.*

That was the other challenge facing Billy and

his friends. Not only did they have to subdue ferocious and furious Dragon Realm creatures, but they also had to find somewhere for them to go. Supercharged pest control *and* removal.

But the world itself was changing as entire landscapes from the Dragon Realm fell into it. Maps were becoming more outdated every day. Billy's hope was that once the whole Dragon Realm had collapsed into the Human Realm, there would somehow be enough space for everyone. He knew that dragons and humans could live peacefully and work together, but creatures like the scorpion were another matter. The humans needed more dragons on their side.

And then, just as Billy thought the scorpion was ready to give up, a flaming fireball the size of a truck tyre fell from the sky and set the creature alight.

Instantly Billy leaped off the scorpion, knowing instinctively that Spark would be there. He landed effortlessly onto her back and watched in horror as more and more fireballs fell from the sky. One nearly singed Xing's tail.

'WHAT'S GOING ON?' Jordan shouted.

'We have to help the scorpion!' Ling-Fei cried. 'Xing! Use your water power!'

'Absolutely not! That awful thing tried to kill both of us. Let it sizzle, I say,' said Xing.

'Xing!' cried Ling-Fei. 'We can't let it suffer like this!'

'Oh, fine,' muttered the dragon, sending out a blast of water to douse the scorpion.

'Wait, are we attacking it or saving it?' said Jordan.

'Saving it, apparently,' said Xing, clearly unimpressed. The now-drenched scorpion hissed in anger and shot a stream of venom at her. She dodged it easily. 'Not that the terrible thing is grateful.'

'I'm sure it's thankful deep inside,' said Ling-Fei. She stroked Xing behind her horns. 'And I'm thankful. You know I hate to see any creature in pain!'

'Even ones who would happily squash you,' said Xing.

'We did the right thing,' said Billy. 'But we do still have a huge angry scorpion on our hands.'

'And these giant flaming fireballs!' added Jordan, as Midnight ducked another one.

Screams rang out from nearby streets as the fireballs continued their onslaught.

'We need more water dragons,' Billy said.

'We need any dragons who are willing to help humans,' said Spark.

'We will help you,' came a new voice, one that echoed in Billy's bones. 'But in return, we need you to help us.'

Diamond Dragons

Billy whirled around to see that an unfamiliar dragon had appeared. Billy was used to encountering new dragons – after all they were arriving every day in the Human Realm now – but this one was different.

It was made of *diamonds*.

Light glinted through its body, refracting and reflecting, and every edge of the creature was sharp and shining. Even its wings looked like sheets of cut glass. But Billy had a feeling they wouldn't shatter the way glass does. No, they'd be stronger than steel. And when the dragon opened its mouth to speak again, Billy saw that even its teeth were diamonds. Only its eyes winked with fire.

Billy knew dragons loved jewels and treasure, but this was something else – this dragon looked as if it had been carved from a block of solid diamond and then brought to life. As he gaped, three more dragons flew out of the smoke, easily dodging the raining fireballs. These were emerald green, ruby red and sapphire blue, their colours winking in the light. They all had different body shapes, but their gleaming gem-scales marked them as linked.

'We will immobilize the scorpion first,' said the ruby dragon. 'As it seems to be the most immediate threat.' It nodded at the sapphire dragon.

The sapphire dragon turned and shot out a jet of bright blue light. As soon as it hit the scorpion, the creature froze, and its skin began to crackle. Moments later, it had hardened into what looked like black diamond. But unlike the diamond dragon, it didn't move.

Everyone stared at it for a few seconds, and then Billy cleared his throat. 'Is it . . . alive?'

'Yes. It is merely locked in a diamond cocoon,' said the emerald dragon. 'It cannot bother you, or anyone, now. We have slowed its heartbeat and put it to sleep so it is not afraid.'

'That's very considerate of you,' said Ling-Fei with a smile.

The emerald dragon turned its gaze to Billy and Spark, and Billy desperately hoped it wasn't about to put *him* in a diamond cocoon. These dragons felt stranger and more ancient than the ones he knew and loved.

Xing and Spark drew together protectively around Midnight, who was watching the gemstone dragons with fascination. 'My mother has jewelled scales,' she said. 'But not like all of you. You don't look like any dragons I've ever seen before.'

Billy was glad that someone had said what he was thinking.

'There are not many of us,' said the ruby dragon. 'But if your mother has jewelled scales, she most likely met our clan and spent time in our mountain. Jewel scales are forged, not born.'

'Your clan?' said Billy. 'What clan is that?'

Unexpectedly, Spark answered. 'The Diamond Clan,' she said, her tone respectful. 'I have heard of your kind, but I did not think I would ever meet you.'

'We do not like to leave our mountain,' said the diamond dragon. 'We would still be there if half of it had not fallen into this realm without warning.'

'Deep in the core of our mountain is a pool of fire, and we believe that when it fell through the realms, it shattered, creating these fireballs,' added the sapphire dragon. 'We can help with those as well.' She threw back her head and roared, and the fireballs paused in mid-air as if frozen.

'Whoa,' breathed Jordan.

'Anything from our mountain will obey us,' the emerald dragon explained. 'And that includes

26

these fireballs. We were forged in our mountain together. Yet we entered it as common dragons . . .'

Xing bristled at the insinuation that she was a common dragon.

'But after centuries inside, well . . .'

'Pressure makes diamonds!' Jordan blurted out. 'It's a saying.'

'It is the truth. Heat and pressure together. We were forged in the hottest flames in the Dragon Realm,' said the ruby dragon, before letting out another tremendous roar. The fireballs pulsed in time, and then each disappeared in a puff of smoke.

The diamond dragon looked at Billy and his friends. 'We have helped you. It is your turn to help us.'

Billy swallowed nervously. It seemed they'd accidentally made a pact without knowing their side of the bargain.

'What is it, exactly, that you need?' said Xing suspiciously. She clearly felt the same way Billy did.

'What we are about to tell you is a secret, kept from dragons and humans alike. We have spent much of our existence protecting something very rare and very dear to us. A dragon egg, entrusted to us by a mother dragon. She sacrificed herself in a battle to protect our mountain. She is a star now, and we believe she watches over us from the skies above. But we have been waiting for many years for the egg to hatch. It is no ordinary dragon egg. It is foretold that the creature born from it will have indescribable power, and the ability to change all the realms.'

Spark gasped and her eyes lit up. 'You speak of the Infinite Dragon. The one dragon who the future of all dragonkind depends on. I have seen this dragon in my visions. Without it there is no future for the dragon world, in this realm or any other.'

The diamond dragon nodded. 'Yes, we know.'

Spark turned to Billy. 'I have seen visions of this dragon with you.'

'But *you* are my dragon . . .' said Billy, bewildered.

He didn't want any dragon other than Spark, no matter how special or powerful it was.

'And I always will be. But you will know this dragon in the future. I believe we both will. We must protect this egg.'

'Wait, where exactly is this magical, super-special egg?' said Jordan.

'Have any of you fallen through the realms unexpectedly? There is no time to prepare when that happens,' said the sapphire dragon.

'I was the one closest to the egg,' said the diamond dragon. 'And I had it safely under my wing when we were pulled from one realm to the other. But as we came through, along with half of our mountain and the pool of fire, the egg became stuck.'

Billy suddenly realized where the egg was. 'The In-Between.'

'Yes,' agreed the diamond dragon, 'and we cannot enter there. We tried to go backwards, but it is not possible. When we fell through, the In-Between did not want us to stay. It pushed us onwards, into your realm, but *something* in there grabbed onto the egg and held on.'

'The realms are growing closer and closer, becoming one,' added the ruby dragon, 'but the In-Between is still a place of both. Now, only those who are from both places are able to enter freely.'

'But nobody is from both realms,' said Jordan.

'Unless . . .' said Billy, as a thought occurred to him, '. . . we count.' He gestured to himself and Spark, Jordan and Midnight and Ling-Fei and Xing. 'With our heart bond, we represent both realms.'

The diamond dragon rewarded him with a dazzlingly bright smile. 'Precisely. We believe you will be able to enter the In-Between. We need you to find our dragon egg before it is lost for ever.'

Bound By Flame

Billy had been in the In-Between three times before.

Once when they had unlocked a magical entrance to the Dragon Realm by answering a tricky riddle.

Then there was the time when Frank Albert had used the *sanguinem gladio* to cut his way into the In-Between and Billy had leaped after him to stop him from destroying both realms. In the battle that followed, the Forbidden Fountain had been sliced open, so that golden elixir flooded the In-Between.

And the final time had been an accident as they'd blasted through the In-Between on their way from the collapsing Dragon Realm. They had only been there for a moment, but it was enough for Billy to see that the golden elixir, which had once been contained within underground rivers and only accessible through the Forbidden Fountain, now flowed freely throughout the In-Between.

And Billy knew anything that came into contact with golden elixir would be for ever changed. A small amount provided power, but too much was dangerous or even deadly.

Billy *really* hoped the dragon egg had managed to land somewhere safe.

'But isn't the In-Between massive?' asked Jordan. 'How will we know where to look?'

Xing let out a sigh. 'I suppose I can help with that. I am a seeker dragon, after all. That is if this egg is even important, which I remain sceptical of.'

'But there's so much magic in the In-Between,'

said Billy thoughtfully. 'Won't that make it hard for you to sense the egg?' He remembered what Spark had told them about the In-Between.

'Between the two realms, there are pockets that exist. Pockets that you can travel to that hold some of the most magical properties in all the lands. Imagine that our realms are held together by a powerful magic, but the seal is not perfect. There are areas where the magic has pooled and bulged and created a pocket that you can visit. These magical pockets between our realms are few and far between, but they exist, and we refer to them simply as the In-Between. The pockets are almost impossible to find.'

Billy suddenly realized Spark was speaking the words aloud so everyone could hear them. He blinked. 'Wait, what just happened?'

Spark smiled at him. 'I could sense what you were trying to remember through our bond, and I was able to unlock the memory since I share it.'

The Diamond Clan watched this exchange with interest.

'The heart bond is strong,' said the emerald

dragon. 'I have not witnessed anything quite like it.'

'If anyone can find the egg, it is you six,' said the ruby dragon.

'I wish Charlotte, Dylan and Lola were here too,' said Ling-Fei. 'We're at our strongest when we're all together.'

Billy missed his other friends too, but he knew they were needed where they were. 'At least the three of us are here,' said Billy. 'And we have our dragons. Together we'll be able to find that egg.'

Jordan grinned at him. 'Always the optimist.'

'If we don't believe we can do it, we never will,' said Billy, grinning back at his friend.

'So you will do it? You will find the egg?' said the diamond dragon.

'We will,' said Billy with as much confidence as he could muster.

'One question. What are we going to do about everything still happening in this realm?' said Jordan, gesturing around at the dragons roaming the streets and the diamond-frozen giant scorpion. 'What happens if something big and scary falls through and we aren't here to help?'

'You are so protective of your realm,' observed the sapphire dragon. 'It is pleasing to see.'

'These are good humans,' said Spark. 'They protect not just those they love, but others who cannot protect themselves.'

'Which is basically all of this world,' said Xing, flicking her tail with annoyance. 'But as I always tell Ling-Fei, we cannot be everywhere, all the time, saving everyone. It is impossible. We need to come up with a better solution, and fast.'

The Diamond Clan all exchanged a long look, and Billy sensed they were communicating in their minds much like he and Spark did.

'We will join you in your fight to protect those who need it,' said the emerald dragon.

'In your effort to bring peace,' added the ruby dragon.

'We will support you, however we can,' said the sapphire dragon.

'But do not disappoint us,' warned the diamond dragon. 'Bring us back our egg, and we will be your allies. Fail, and we will for ever distrust humans.'

Billy gulped. He didn't want to make enemies out of these powerful dragons. The challenge they'd set hung like a heavy weight round his neck.

'But we can't promise we'll be able to find the egg!' said Jordan, sounding panicked. 'I've been to the In-Between, and there's all sorts there. I know this egg is super important, but anything could have happened to it.'

'Then for all of your sakes, let us hope that something good has befallen our precious egg,' said the diamond dragon, and Billy could have sworn its jewelled teeth had grown sharper.

'It's a deal,' he said, holding out his hand. Xing was right. They were overwhelmed by so many dangerous creatures falling into their realm and needed as many dragons on their side as possible.

Once upon a time, Billy had followed four dragons into the unknown because they said they needed him to save two realms. Now, Billy knew he'd do anything to protect the single merged realm.

'Humans and their handshakes,' said Xing. 'You should know by now that means nothing to a dragon.'

'Blood and flame,' Jordan said under his breath. 'Always blood and flame.'

'No,' said the diamond dragon. 'We do not demand your blood. Not yet.' It gave another sharp-toothed smile. 'Your word will be enough. All of you humans, say it together. Say you will find the egg.'

Billy, Jordan and Ling-Fei exchanged a hesitant look.

'We are waiting,' said the diamond dragon.

'We will find the egg,' the three friends chorused. As they spoke the words, Billy felt a sharp sting on his arm. He looked down and gasped.

Cursive words he didn't recognize were inked in black on his arm.

Alligatus flamma

'Alligator something? What is that?' asked Jordan, sounding as confused as Billy felt.

'It is in Latin – the human tongue that is closest to our language,' said the emerald dragon.

'Where's Dylan when we need him?' said Billy. Dylan loved languages, and he had immediately known that *sanguinem gladio* meant blood sword.

'It means bound by flame,' Spark spoke softly. 'There was no need for blood to be spilled for this to be a vow bound by flame and blood.'

Billy exhaled, realizing that they couldn't get out of this now even if they wanted to.

'We can do it, Billy,' whispered Ling-Fei. 'We just mustn't lose faith in ourselves.'

'We are now bound by our word too,' said the ruby dragon. 'We will protect this world as well as we can. And when you return, with the egg, perhaps we can be convinced to continue to help you and the rest of humanity.'

The words bolstered Billy. He turned to his friends and their dragons. 'Right. Time to find that egg.'

Back To The In-Between

'One more question,' said Jordan. 'What are you going to do with *that* thing?' He pointed down at the giant scorpion still stuck in the diamond cocoon.

'The landscape in this realm has changed significantly,' said the ruby dragon.

'We noticed,' Billy said dryly.

'There are new islands, new oceans, new lands, including an island that is perfectly habitable for creatures of the Arachnida group,' said the sapphire dragon.

'Arachnida? Like … arachnid? Like spiders?' asked Billy, repressing a shudder. He'd never told his friends, but he hated spiders.

'Precisely. When we tumbled into this realm, we saw that exact island fall in after us. We will take the scorpion there in its diamond form and then release it.'

'But what will it eat?' asked Ling-Fei.

Jordan scoffed. 'It's a giant magical scorpion! It'll eat anything it wants!'

Midnight let out a laugh. 'Jordan's right. The scorpion will be fine.'

'Enough worrying about the wretched scorpion,' said Xing. 'If we must rescue this egg, we should do it soon. More of the Dragon Realm is collapsing into our realm with every passing second, and who knows what is coming with it.'

Billy grinned at her, and Xing scowled back. 'Why are you smiling at me?'

'You said "our realm",' he said. 'You see this one as your home now too.'

'Aw, Xing! That's so sweet!' said Ling-Fei, stroking her dragon's head.

Spark let out a snort that Billy was pretty sure was a suppressed laugh.

'Oh, be quiet. All of you! Of all the times to be sentimental,' Xing grumbled.

Spark turned to the Diamond Clan. 'You must have fallen in from somewhere nearby,' she said.

'Them and the rest of the creatures from the old realm,' muttered Xing, clearly still disgruntled. 'Everything is coming our way and giving us trouble.'

'We did indeed,' said the emerald dragon. 'Far higher than here, of course.'

'Xing should be able to find the spot you entered with her seeker power, and I will be able to open a portal to the In-Between,' replied Spark. 'But we will not have a connection to the egg. Ling-Fei, we will be depending on you and Xing.'

Ling-Fei flushed with pride. 'I won't let you down. Any of you.'

Billy leaned over from Spark to clap his friend

on the back. 'I know you won't,' he said. 'All right, Spark, are you ready to open a portal?'

'Of course I am,' said Spark. 'That is my specialty.' She looked at Xing. 'Xing, lead us to the tear in the sky.'

Xing shot off into the sky, zigzagging back and forth, clearly trying to locate the spot.

'Wait for us!' cried Midnight, zooming after Xing with Jordan on her back.

'Do not disappoint us,' said the diamond dragon to Billy and Spark.

'We won't,' said Billy firmly. He felt the thrill of a quest sparking in his blood, and the joy of knowing he would be with his dragon and his friends. Together, they could achieve anything. With one final nod to the Diamond Clan, Spark followed, and Billy leaned into the wind and the adventure ahead.

By the time Billy and Spark had caught up with Xing, the silver dragon had found what they were looking for.

'It is here,' she said, wrinkling her snout.

'Something is pouring out of it. Something powerful. It smells like magic. At first, I thought it was golden elixir, but only the smell is in the air.'

'Perhaps the golden elixir turns from liquid into gas when it enters this realm,' Spark suggested. 'But we can reflect on that after we have found the egg. I will make the portal.'

Billy sensed Spark gearing up to create a portal, and he channelled his own power into her, helping to make her stronger. Spark focused her eyes on the spot Xing had indicated, and moments later a swirling silver-and-blue hole opened in the sky.

'That is it,' said Xing, almost in awe. 'There is more magic flowing out of that portal right now than I have ever encountered. It will lead us to the In-Between.'

'See you there!' piped Midnight. 'Come on, Jordan!' They flew through and disappeared. Xing and Ling-Fei followed, and then it was just Billy and Spark.

'Hold on!' said Spark.

Entering a portal felt like being shot through

a straw – squished flat and then inflated again. The feeling was nearly unbearable, but it was over in less than a second. Then Spark tumbled tail over snout into the dim glow of the In-Between.

'Everyone here?' Billy called out.

'Made it!' said Midnight.

'Where else would we be?' said Xing drolly.

'Well done on the portal, Spark,' said Jordan. 'But now what do we do?'

Now that he knew his friends were all safe, Billy turned his head to see where they had landed. Below them was a long and winding stone bridge which he remembered, but everything else was different. Previously, there had been a sparkling body of water, dark and still and fathomless, beneath the bridge. That was gone. In its place was a frothing, bubbling river of golden liquid, sloshing up onto the bridge. And where the liquid made contact, the bridge disintegrated.

That wasn't the only difference. Once a thick fog had blanketed everything, with a swirling darkness dotted with glittering light beyond it. But now the air was full of crackling energy, as if there was static electricity everywhere. There was a small *pop* next to Billy, and he jolted with surprise. It was almost as if they were floating amongst thousands of tiny crackling fireworks, all going off at once. At the edges of the In-Between, Billy could see cracks. And running through the cracks was more bright gold liquid.

Golden elixir. It was everywhere.

'That is what was seeping through into the Human Realm,' said Xing. 'Less concentrated, but it is the same odour. Ling-Fei, do you smell it too?'

Ling-Fei nodded and swayed a little on Xing's back. 'It's so powerful, it's making me feel dizzy. Every breath I take, I can feel it filling my lungs. We shouldn't stay here for long.'

'Well, obviously . . .' said Jordan.

'Xing, can you sense the egg anywhere?' asked Spark.

'You heard Ling-Fei,' Xing snapped. 'My senses

are overwhelmed as well. It feels like I am trying to smell a rose petal in a bowl of pepper.'

Billy felt his stomach twist with nerves. He hadn't considered what they would do if Ling-Fei and Xing couldn't sense the egg. The In-Between was nearly impossible to navigate, especially with golden elixir flowing through it.

Then Billy had an idea. 'Ling-Fei, you need Xing to supercharge you.'

'What a preposterous statement,' said Xing.

'You know what I mean,' said Billy. 'Spark did it for me, back when we were battling the scorpion and it was about to turn you into dragon mulch.'

Xing rolled her eyes. 'Charming. But, yes, I did mean to thank you for saving us.'

'No problem,' said Billy. 'But I was only able to do it because Spark supercharged me. I think you can do the same with Ling-Fei.'

'Can Midnight supercharge me?' said Jordan.

'Of course! If the others can do it, so can I!' said Midnight. She was obviously eager to prove that she could keep up with the older, more experienced dragons.

'Okay, Xing . . . supercharge me!' said Ling-Fei and shut her eyes tight in anticipation.

Xing went very still, and then she began to glow silver. And to Billy's amazement, Ling-Fei began to glow too. They both kept shining until they were so bright that Billy had to shield his eyes, but when he looked again Ling-Fei was glowing faintly, as if she'd been dusted by starlight.

'I can hear *everything*,' she whispered. 'Everything! Your heartbeats! All of them!' Then she paused and tilted her head to the side, concentrating. 'And there are other heartbeats too. There are other living creatures in here!'

'Well, I'd personally like to avoid all of them if we can,' said Jordan a little uneasily. 'Except for the egg, of course.'

'Ling-Fei, can you sense the egg? It is very powerful. It should call to you,' said Spark.

Ling-Fei closed her eyes. 'Something is calling to me, and whatever it is, it's bursting with power.'

'Then we follow it,' said Billy firmly. 'Ling-Fei, lead the way.'

As Ling-Fei and Xing led the group through twisty tunnels, it felt as if they were going deeper and deeper inside the In-Between. Cracks laced the walls, and Billy worried the place could collapse on itself at any moment.

They went on and on, until Xing suddenly stopped and lifted her head up to peer at the nearest crack.

'Is the egg in there?' whispered Midnight.

'I don't think so,' said Ling-Fei, nudging Xing onwards. 'I think it's this way, though. We're getting closer.'

'Wait,' said Xing, her voice deadly serious. 'Something is wrong.'

Then she quickly whipped her head up. 'GET BACK! GET BACK! SPARK! MIDNIGHT! MAKE US A SHIELD! NOW!'

As Spark and Midnight combined powers to create a glowing orb around the three dragons and their riders, Billy saw the crack Xing had been investigating start to bulge as if something was pressing on it from the other side. It widened and its edges grew fuzzy. Through it, they could see the shadow of something hurtling towards them.

'Something is falling from the Dragon Realm into the Human Realm, and it's passing through the In-Between,' whispered Ling-Fei.

'I hope it's not something that wants to eat us,' said Jordan.

'It will most likely fall through too fast to see us,' said Xing.

'And we are protected by our shield,' added Spark.

'I make really excellent shields,' said Midnight, puffing out her chest with pride.

Moments later, something tumbled through the crack. It was in shadow, but Billy could tell it was multi-limbed with long sharp claws and covered in magical orbs ... Wait a second. Were those *peaches*?

'It's a peach tree!' cried Ling-Fei.

It was indeed one of the famed Peach Trees of the Dragon Realm. They were practically indestructible and while most of their fruit was normal, sometimes they grew Peaches of Immortality. It was impossible to tell which ones they were, and it would obviously take a long time to find out, but it did make eating peaches in the Dragon Realm much more exciting.

Four more peach trees fell after the first, their roots sticking up in every direction. The peaches shook with the impact but, remarkably, stayed on their branches.

Billy let out a low whistle. 'Peaches of Immortality in the Human Realm. Wild.'

'I bet some humans would do anything to become immortal,' said Jordan.

Billy frowned. 'I don't think we should tell people the peaches can do that,' he said. 'Though if someone does eat a Peach of Immortality, well, they'll figure it out eventually.'

They watched another three trees tumble in and then out of the In-Between, then the crack they had come through seemed to stretch before snapping shut. It faded, like it was disappearing right before Billy's eyes. He swallowed. He didn't want to be caught here when the In-Between disappeared for good.

'All right,' he said to his friends. 'Let's find that egg before something falls right on top of us.'

'We're close, I think,' said Ling-Fei. 'The heartbeat is getting louder.'

'Midnight, Spark, let down the shield,' said Jordan. The glowing orb around them popped like a bubble, and they continued through the In-Between.

The tunnel Ling-Fei and Xing turned down next was narrow. So narrow it was difficult for Spark to fit, and almost impossible for her to fly because she could barely open her wings.

'There!' cried Ling-Fei, pointing ahead. 'The egg! I can feel it calling me!'

'Wait for us!' said Billy. 'Just in case something else is in there too. We should be together.'

The tunnel opened out into a small cavern.

A small cavern that was completely empty. Not a dragon egg in sight.

The Oracle Ox

'Is it an *invisible* egg?' asked Jordan.

Billy glanced up at Ling-Fei. 'Can you still feel something calling to you, Ling-Fei?'

Ling-Fei looked close to tears. 'I don't know. Something in here was calling me, but now it's gone silent.' She sighed. 'Maybe I've led us the wrong way, but I was so certain.'

Instinctively, Billy reached out and grabbed Ling-Fei's hand, and then Jordan's. He felt a familiar surge of power ricochet between them, and the air began to hum. Billy knew he and his friends were strongest when they were together, and sometimes they could amplify their powers by joining hands, almost as if an electric current was shared between them.

Suddenly, the cavern wall in front of them shattered, revealing a cave full of bones. And in the middle, on a raised platform, was an ox made of gold.

'Er ... did we just explode that wall with our powers? And, more importantly, do you guys see that golden ox?' whispered Jordan.

'How could we miss it?' Billy said. His head was spinning. This wasn't what they had been looking for, yet it felt like they were on the right path.

Ling-Fei was watching the ox very carefully. 'It's alive,' she said.

The golden ox opened its eyes, and they were like two stars staring out at them.

'An oracle,' Xing whispered, in the most deferential tone Billy had ever heard her use.

Midnight let out a loud squeak of excitement, and Spark bowed her head respectfully.

'Why have you woken me?' said the ox. Its voice was like thunder, echoing all around them and rattling the bones on the ground. 'What do you seek? Your future? Your fortune? Your fate? Humans always want something.'

'We did not mean to disturb you,' said Xing. 'We are seeking an egg.'

'I know this, of course,' said the golden ox. 'But I also know what will happen if you find this egg.' Its gaze sharpened. 'The In-Between is vanishing. Too much golden elixir flows, and too freely. Creatures are still passing through as they fall from the Dragon Realm into the Human Realm but none can return here. Only those of both realms, such as heart-bonded dragons and humans like yourselves, can do so. But I warn you – if you re-enter the Human Realm, and bring the egg with you, it will be like pulling on the last thread. It will trigger the Great Collapse. The whole Dragon Realm will fall into the Human Realm, all at once.'

'That sounds dangerous,' said Billy. 'What are our other options?'

The golden ox flared its nostrils. 'You stay here, in the In-Between, for eternity.'

'That's it? Those are our choices?' said Billy, feeling his palms begin to sweat.

'That is it. I am an oracle. I see everything that can happen. All versions of the future. And there are only two options for you three humans and your three dragons. Eternity here, or causing the Great Collapse of the realms.'

Billy cleared his throat. 'Technically, the realms are already collapsing. We wouldn't be causing it exactly . . .' His voice trailed off.

'You *would* be causing the Great Collapse – the final collapse of the Dragon Realm into the Human Realm, resulting, of course, in a new world entirely. It is your choice.'

The golden ox closed its eyes, as though the conversation had ended.

'But if you're an oracle, can't you see what we're going to do?' asked Jordan.

'No, I can see possibilities. I do not know which road you will take,' said the ox.

'So you're kind of like Spark,' said Billy. 'My dragon. She's a seer dragon.'

The ox's eyes flashed open. 'No, a seer dragon has visions of *a* future. I see all.'

Spark spoke quickly. 'An oracle such as this one is much more skilled at divining the future than seer dragons. As you know, my visions can be cloudy. An oracle can see much more clearly. Every version of the future is available to them to see in clarity.'

The ox nodded in approval. 'Exactly.'

'Can you tell us where the egg is?' said Billy. 'You must know.'

'I do indeed. Is that the course you wish to take?'

'Well, I don't want to be stuck in here for ever,' said Billy. 'No offence.'

Suddenly, the golden ox let out a loud guffaw. 'Of course. But you would grow very powerful here, with so much golden elixir everywhere. Powerful and strange.'

'Our realm needs us,' said Billy firmly. 'We need to find the egg and return home.'

'Very well.' The ox stood up, its powerful muscles rippling. It moved like liquid, and Billy wondered if it was made entirely of golden elixir.

With its hooves, the ox cleared away one of the piles of bones, revealing a stone slab. It used its snout to push the slab aside. A glow filled the room, and Billy heard the rush of a fast-moving river – a river of golden elixir.

The ox straightened up and stared at them with its too-bright eyes. 'This is the only way to find the egg,' it said. 'Jump in here, and you will be taken to it.'

'But that's pure golden elixir,' protested Billy. 'We might not survive.'

'You will,' said the ox simply. 'I have seen it. In no version of the future do you drown here.'

'But what will happen to us?' said Ling-Fei.

'That I cannot tell you. But you will find the egg. And if you take it out of the In-Between, you will cause the Great Collapse. It is all up to you.'

Billy took a deep breath. 'We have to try,' he said. 'I say we take the risk.' They had to be brave; it was the only way to move forward. And he couldn't focus on his fear or it would suffocate him. Instead, he gripped onto hope.

'I'm in,' said Jordan.

'Me too,' said Ling-Fei.

'We will be with you,' said Spark. 'No matter what happens.'

'How will our dragons even fit?' said Jordan, eyeing the square that the ox had revealed.

'The dragons will fit,' said the ox. 'Your eyes deceive you. It looks as if the entrance is human-sized, but the dragons will see an entrance big enough for them.'

'This place is so weird,' muttered Jordan.

Billy looked at the Oracle Ox. 'Thank you for pointing us in the right direction.'

'I merely showed you the options,' said the ox. Then its mouth curved into a smile. 'And I will see you all again, in your world, one day.'

And with that, it returned to its raised chair and closed its eyes before it went as still as a statue again. Billy found himself grinning back at the golden ox. He had the strangest feeling that they'd just made a very unlikely friend.

'Well,' said Billy, looking down at the rushing river of golden elixir. 'Here we go.' He jumped in, hoping for the best.

The Spidragon

The golden elixir was thick. Billy felt like he was being pulled down into a river of honey. He kept his eyes and mouth tightly shut, but as he felt the liquid pouring into his ears and his nose, he had to tell himself not to panic. The Oracle Ox had said they wouldn't drown.

Billy felt a strange fizzing inside his skin, like the golden elixir was sinking into his pores and his blood, changing him somehow. But he wouldn't let himself be afraid. At least that's what he thought until the river shot him out into a huge sticky web and he found himself staring up at the most terrifying sight he'd ever seen.

An eight-legged, eight-eyed monster was staring back at him. It had the head of a dragon and the mouth of a giant spider, with pincers protruding out of it. Its eight legs clacked as it scuttled upside down across the stone ceiling above the web where Billy was stuck. The web bounced as Jordan landed in it, and then Ling-Fei, and then the three dragons.

'What is THAT?' said Jordan.

'That is a spidragon,' said Xing grimly. 'A cross between a dragon and a spider. I thought they were extinct.'

'Well, nobody told that one it's supposed to be extinct,' said Jordan.

Billy was so petrified he couldn't even speak. All he could do was stare at the huge spidragon as it crept closer and closer to them. For some reason, spiders always made his skin crawl. He could battle giant scorpions, face down dragons, scale the highest buildings, but spiders creeped him out. Especially now he was caught in the web of a giant one.

The ox had said they wouldn't drown, but it had said nothing about not being devoured by a horrifying spidragon straight out of Billy's worst nightmares.

'Look!' cried Ling-Fei. 'In the web up there! The egg! I can sense it!'

Billy tore his gaze away from the spidragon, and then he saw it – a glowing golden egg. Despite everything, he was filled with hope. They'd found it. They'd found the egg containing the Infinite Dragon. The dragon that their future depended on.

'Spark! Can you get the egg?'

Spark shook her head. 'This is no ordinary web. It blocks my powers, and it has a fast-acting poison in it that affects dragons. You see, the spidragon is hated among dragonkind because it eats its own. It is probably waiting for the egg to hatch, to devour it.'

Billy thought he might throw up at the very thought.

'But what about our powers?' said Ling-Fei. 'I can still sense everything.'

'Humans don't usually have powers,' said Billy. 'So maybe the poison isn't affecting us!' He tried and failed to wriggle out of the web's sticky grip.

'But the stickiness is,' said Xing with an uncharacteristic pessimism. 'We are trapped. All of us.'

'There has to be *something* we can do!' declared Midnight. 'I refuse to be a spider's lunch!'

'I could try to talk to it?' Ling-Fei suggested tentatively. 'Using my nature power?'

'Spidragons have no empathy,' said Spark quietly. 'It will not listen to you.'

'But we have to try!' cried Billy as the spidragon crept even closer.

'WAIT!' shouted Jordan. 'I KNOW!' He tilted his head until it was touching Midnight's wing. 'One . . . two . . .'

And Jordan and Midnight teleported out of the web.

The spidragon let out an indignant hiss as it saw

part of its meal disappear. A moment later, Jordan and Midnight popped back into sight, right in front of the dragon egg.

'I've got it!' Jordan cried, reaching out and tugging the precious egg out of the web.

The spidragon quickly changed direction, crawling faster than Billy thought any creature should be able to crawl, up towards where Jordan and Midnight hovered.

Still clutching the egg, Jordan teleported back to where Billy and the others were. 'Billy, hold the egg! I'll teleport everyone else out of the web!'

And moments later, Jordan had done it – the dragons were free, and so was Ling-Fei. Billy was the only one still in the web, holding the egg to his chest.

Realizing what had happened, the spidragon let itself fall, aiming directly for Billy and the egg. Billy closed his eyes, preparing for eight legs to close around him. Everything was happening so fast that he didn't even have time to be afraid, all he could think about was protecting the egg.

Suddenly, there was a flash of light and power, and the spidragon froze, still dangling from its thread. Spark had blasted it with her powers and turned it into ice.

'Do not worry. It will thaw eventually,' said Spark.

'I wasn't worried,' said Billy with a weak grin. 'But can someone please get me out of this web?'

The Great Collapse

After Jordan had teleported Billy out of the web, there was only one thing left to do ... return to the Human Realm.

Billy, Jordan and Ling-Fei sat on the backs of their dragons. Billy clutched the dragon egg they had come into the In-Between for, nearly losing their lives in the process. But they had done it. They'd saved the dragon egg and they'd survived.

'I will open a portal for us back into the Human Realm,' said Spark. 'But remember what the Oracle Ox said.'

'The Great Collapse sounds pretty epic,' said Jordan. 'I just hope the Human Realm is ready for everything that's going to come from the Dragon Realm.'

'We'll be there to help,' said Billy. 'And we have the Diamond Clan on our side now. Other dragons will join us too, I'm sure of it. Humans and dragons can get along, and we'll build a world, a new world, where we can all live peacefully, protecting each other from whatever may come.'

'I'm ready,' said Ling-Fei.

'Then it is settled,' said Xing. 'Spark, prepare the portal.'

The portal Spark opened was gold and swirling, and Billy knew that it had golden elixir mixed in it. That magical liquid would soon be in the Human Realm, and who knew what would happen? But whatever was in store, whatever the Oracle Ox had seen in their future, he was ready for it.

As they leaped into the portal, leaving the In-Between behind, Billy felt it.

A rumbling.

The Great Collapse was beginning.

It was the start of a brand-new adventure for them all.

WORLD
**BOOK
DAY**
2 MARCH 2023

Happy
World Book Day!

When you've read this book, you can keep the fun going by: swapping it, talking about it with a friend, or reading it again!

What do you want to read next? Whether it's **comics**, **audiobooks**, **recipe books** or **non-fiction,** you can visit your school, local library or nearest bookshop for your next read – someone will always be happy to help.

World Book Day is about changing lives through reading

When children **choose to read** in their spare time it makes them

Feel happier	Better at reading	More successful

Help the children in your lives **make the choice to read** by:

1. **Reading to them**
2. **Having books at home**
3. **Letting them choose what they want to read**
4. **Helping them choose what they want to read**
5. **Making time for reading**
6. **Making reading fun!**

SPONSORED BY

Changing lives through a love of books and reading
World Book Day® is a charity sponsored by National Book Tokens

Illustration Allen Fatimaharan

Have you read all the
DRAGON REALM
books?

Read on for an exciting
extract from

DRAGON
MOUNTAIN

Billy Chan was certain of two things. He had great hair and he was the best surfer in the 11–14 age bracket in all of California.

He did not think either of those things were going to help him in his current situation. He was by himself. On a train platform. Somewhere in middle-of-nowhere China. The train ride had felt like for ever. He didn't even know what time it was. He reached into his pocket and gripped his lucky seashell. At least he had a small piece of home with him.

All around him were huge mountains wrapped in green foliage, climbing to dizzying heights. Even the

Hong Kong skyscrapers he'd seen just a few days ago would have looked tiny here.

The only indication of *exactly* where in China he might be was written in peeling, faded yellow Chinese characters above the station doorway. Chinese characters that Billy couldn't read.

He really, really hoped he was in the right place.

Billy looked around, trying to find the staff for the summer camp he was going to. The summer camp his parents were forcing him to go to so he could 'improve his Mandarin' and 'learn more about his Chinese heritage'. Even though what Billy *wanted* to do all summer was go surfing with his friends.

He did not see any camp staff. The only people nearby were two old Chinese women playing mahjong on a rickety table, cackling as they swirled the green tiles around.

'Hello?' he called out. '*Ni hao?*'

One of the old women looked up and waved him towards the tiny station.

Billy nodded his thanks and went inside, dragging his suitcase behind him.

Billy's eyes took a moment to adjust to the dimness inside the station after the blisteringly bright sun outside. He breathed a sigh of relief. Clustered around the room were about a dozen kids his age.

A slightly older Chinese boy with slicked-back black hair sauntered over, holding a clipboard. He looked Billy up and down, and appeared distinctly unimpressed.

'You must be Billy Chan,' he said.

Billy nodded.

The boy sighed deeply, as if meeting Billy was the most annoying thing that had happened to him all day. 'Finally,' he said. 'It took you long enough to get here.'

Billy flushed. He was already off to a terrible start. 'Well, this place is a *really* long way away from California. And my train was delayed . . .'

'*Ni shuo putonghua ma?*' the boy interrupted, his eyebrow raised.

Billy paused. He understood the boy was asking him if he spoke Mandarin, and he realized he said this as a challenge.

'*Yi dian dian,*' he replied, being careful to get

his pronunciation right of the phrase meaning 'a little bit'.

The older boy frowned. 'I guess you're not as Chinese as your name suggests, Billy *Chan*.'

Billy was used to this. Used to people trying to figure out where he was from. He knew what the boy wanted to know. 'My dad is Chinese. From Hong Kong. And my mom is white,' he explained. 'My parents sent me to this camp to improve my Mandarin.' He tried to keep the bitterness out of his voice. He still hadn't forgiven his parents for making him spend his whole summer at a language culture camp in China. He looked at the other kids, who seemed to have gathered round them. 'That's why we're all here, right?'

The responding nods and smiles made him feel slightly reassured.

'Whatever,' said the older boy, sounding bored.

'And who are you?' said Billy, summoning as much confidence in his voice as he could muster.

The boy looked down his nose at Billy. 'I'm JJ. My grandfather runs the camp.'

'Got it, boss,' said Billy, hoping JJ would pick up

on his sarcasm. Billy made a note to avoid him at all costs.

Just then, a wizened old Chinese man with a long white beard burst into the station, moving quickly, considering his age. He looked ancient, as if he'd stepped out of the past.

'Welcome, everyone! I'm the head of the camp. It is a pleasure to meet you all. You can call me Jin *laoshi*.'

A short girl with long blonde hair, almost to her waist, shot her hand up in the air. 'As in "Gold Teacher"?' She had a southern accent. Billy thought she must be from somewhere like Alabama.

The old man laughed. 'Yes! I can tell someone already knows a bit of Mandarin.'

Billy wished *he* had remembered that *laoshi* meant teacher. It was one of the first things he'd learned at Chinese school back home in San Francisco. He was hit by a wave of worry that everyone here was going to be better than he was. And, to make things worse, the other students might expect him to be really good just because he was part-Chinese. It didn't matter that his dad's side of the family was from

Hong Kong and they spoke Cantonese, a different dialect of Chinese. He looked around at the eager faces of the other kids. They all seemed happy to be here. His palms started to sweat and his neck felt hot. He wished he could jump back on the train and then a plane and go all the way home again.

'You can simply call me Lao Jin or Old Gold,' the old man went on. 'You aren't required to speak Mandarin outside your language classes. But I'll explain all that when we get to camp. Now come with me,' he said. 'Our adventure is about to begin.'

Billy followed Old Gold and the others into the parking lot where a faded yellow-and-green van waited. Billy thought the car looked at least twice as old as him. Old Gold flung the door open, revealing two rows of six seats, like a miniature bus.

Billy clambered in and sat at the back. A boy with short brown hair, glasses and more freckles than Billy had ever seen on anyone flopped into the seat next to him, breathing heavily.

'It is *hot* here,' he said, wiping his brow. His green eyes were wide behind his glasses. 'I'm Dylan O'Donnell, by the way.' He stuck out his hand. Billy stared. He'd never seen someone his age introduce themselves with a handshake.

Billy blinked at the boy, trying to place his accent. It wasn't American, and it wasn't British, but it seemed strangely familiar.

'Um, hi. I'm Billy Chan,' said Billy, awkwardly shaking Dylan's hand.

'Nice to meet you! I've got a cousin named Billy,' said Dylan, grinning as if this was a very interesting fact.

'Cool,' said Billy. 'Er, I don't know anyone named Dylan.'

'Pleasure to be the first!'

The van revved to life and, with a start, hurtled forward.

'Seat belts, everyone!' shouted Old Gold from the front.

'So, where are you from?' asked Billy, still trying to place Dylan's accent.

'The Emerald Isle! Land of saints and scholars! Home of poets! And yes, a lot of sheep.' He said this last bit with a wry grin, as if he was making a joke.

Billy stared at him, still confused. Dylan sighed.

'Ireland. I'm from Ireland.'

Billy wracked his brain and tried to remember if he knew anything about Ireland. 'Dublin?' he attempted.

'I'm from the west coast, actually. Galway. It's by the sea.' Dylan's voice went up an octave as the van flew round a corner.

Billy's stomach churned as the van swayed, but he took a deep breath and tried to keep his cool. 'Are you a surfer?' he asked Dylan, glad that his own voice stayed steady as the van took another wild turn.

Dylan laughed. He had a musical laugh, the kind you'd want to keep listening to long after it stopped.

'Me?' he said. 'Oh, no. Too many jellyfish. And I burn easily, even in Ireland.'

Billy tried to keep from visibly wilting. His suspicions about not having anything in common with the other kids at camp were right so far.

'Do *you* surf?' asked Dylan.

Billy nodded.

'Cowabunga, dude!' said Dylan in an atrocious American accent, making the hang-loose sign with his left hand. He grinned, showing a gap between his two front teeth, and Billy found himself grinning back despite himself.

As they zoomed along narrow, winding roads, Old Gold rolled down the window and howled with glee.

Billy looked out of the window, watching the world hurtle by. Amidst flashes of green foliage and pockets of blue sky were glimpses of jagged yellow cliffs and stony peaks. Every time they swerved, he tensed, certain the van was going to tumble down into the ravines below.

He imagined the headline in the local news at home: Local Surf Champion Plummets to Death in China. He bet his parents would be sorry then for sending him here all summer.

Dylan was clearly feeling the same way. 'Going a bit fast, aren't we?' he said, looking panicked.

'My older brother likes to race cars,' said a girl with long blonde hair, the one who had known what *laoshi* meant. 'So this is totally normal to me.' Her pale face said otherwise. 'I might even be a race-car driver one day.'

'If we survive this journey, you mean,' said Dylan, looking a little green.

Even though Billy had been thinking the exact same thing, he put on what he hoped was a reassuring smile. 'I'm sure we're fine,' he said.

Right then, there was a thump and a scratch as a large branch hit the side of the van.

'Just a tree!' Old Gold hollered. 'Nothing to worry about!'

The van whizzed on higher and higher and the landscape changed. Every bump in the road – and there were a lot – sent the van flying, giving Billy that same weightless feeling he got on roller coasters. They wound up and up until they were level with the clouds, and then . . .

'Whoa,' breathed Billy. They were inside a cloud. All around them was a grey fog.

'I can't see anything!' screeched Dylan. "How can Old Gold see where he's going?'

'Don't worry,' called Old Gold. 'I can do this drive with my eyes closed!'

'Please don't!' Dylan cried back.

Old Gold just laughed.

KATIE & KEVIN TSANG met in 2008 while studying at the Chinese University of Hong Kong. Since then they have lived on three different continents and travelled to over 40 countries together. As well as the DRAGON REALM series, they are the co-writers of the young fiction series SAM WU IS NOT AFRAID (Egmont) and SPACE BLASTERS (Farshore) and Katie also writes YA as Katherine Webber.

And there are even more
dragon books coming soon
with the launch of

DRAGON FORCE

September 2023

They rumbled on, and with a sudden burst of sunshine they were through the cloud cover and above it.

Billy was certain that if they went any higher they'd be able to touch the sky. In the distance he could see even higher mountain peaks, their jagged points covered in snow.

'Is the camp on top of a cliff?' asked the blonde girl.

'It's over this mountain,' said JJ. 'We're almost there.'

The van zoomed down a steep incline, plunging them back into the cloud cover, and then out again, but instead of jagged cliff faces they were now surrounded by trees in every direction. Billy thought he glimpsed a waterfall, but they were going too fast for him to tell.

As the trees opened up into a clearing, with a collection of small cabins scattered around, the van screeched to a stop, flinging them all forward against their seat belts.

The van door slid open, showering them in sunlight.

'Welcome to Camp Dragon,' said Old Gold.